Just So Stories

How the Leopard got his Spots

Miles Kelly

There was once a leopard
who had a yellowish-brownish
coat. Everything around him...

the grass

the rocks

the animals

...was a
yellowish-brownish
colour too.

The leopard was hardest to spot, so it was easy for him to sneak up on other animals and **eat them for dinner!**

The leopard would hide behind a yellowish-brownish rock, or lie in the tall yellowish-brownish grass. Then he would

leap out!

Yikes!

Sometimes the leopard hunted with his friend the man. Then the other animals didn't know which way to jump!

So bit by bit (the giraffe began it, because his legs were the longest) the animals scuttled off to find a place to hide.

At last they came to a great forest. The trees and bushes cast **stripy, speckly** shadows.

After a long time of standing with the slippery, slidy shadows falling on them, the giraffe grew blotchy and the zebra grew stripy and the antelope grew darker.

At last you could hear them and smell them, but you could hardly see them at all.

Meanwhile, the leopard and the man were looking all over their yellowish-brownish home, wondering where all their breakfasts and lunches and dinners had gone!

So the leopard and the man went to see the baboon, who was quite the wisest animal they knew. The leopard asked, "Where has our breakfast gone?"

The baboon said to the man, "My friend, your breakfast decided it was time for a change. You should change, too."

Then the baboon winked, and said, "Leopard, your breakfast has gone into other spots. You should do the same."

So the leopard and the man set off to look for their breakfast. At last they came to a great forest, full of **spotty, dotty** shadows.

"What is this?" asked the leopard. "I can **hear** zebra, and I can **smell** zebra, but I can't **see** zebra."

"It's strange," agreed the man. "I can hear giraffe, and I can smell giraffe, but I can't see giraffe."

That night, the leopard heard something moving in the dark, so he jumped on top of it. It felt like zebra. It smelled like zebra.

CRASH!

He heard the man catch something too. They decided to sit on these strange, invisible things until morning.

In the morning they looked at what they had caught. The man said, "Mine looks like giraffe, but it is covered with brown blotches."

Leopard said, "Mine looks like zebra, but it is covered with black stripes. What have you been doing zebra? Why is it so hard to find you?"

"Let us up," said the zebra, "and we'll show you." So they did. The zebra walked to some bushes where the sunlight fell all stripy. The giraffe walked to some trees where the shadows fell all blotchy.

"Now, where's your breakfast?"

Leopard looked, and the man looked, but they could see only **stripy, blotchy** shadows. "That's a trick worth learning," said the leopard.

"The long and the short of it is, we don't match our backgrounds," said the man. "The baboon told me to change, so I'm going to change my skin." So he changed his skin there and then.

"Well you can't stay as you are," said the man. "You stand out in this forest like a bar of soap in a coal pit!" So the leopard agreed.

"Just don't make them too big, like giraffe!"

So the man put his fingers close together and pressed them on the leopard's fur. Wherever they touched they left five little marks, close together. You can see them today on any leopard's skin you like.

"Now look at you!" said the man. "You can lie on the bare ground and look like a **heap of pebbles**.

You can lie on a branch and look like **sunshine through the leaves.**

You can lie right across a path and look like **nothing in particular.** Those animals will never see you coming!"

So the leopard went away and lived **happily ever after.** That is all!

Purrrrr!